The Donkey
hat Was
'oo Fast

First published 2005
Evans Brothers Limited
2A Portman Mansions
Chiltern St
London W1U 6NR

British Library Cataloguing in Publication Data
Orme, David
        The donkey that was too fast. – (Zig zag)
        1. Children's stories – Pictorial works
        I. Title
        823.9'14 [J]

ISBN 0237529491
13-digit ISBN (from 1 January 2007) 9780237529499

Printed in China by WKT Company Ltd

Series Editor: Nick Turpin
Design: Robert Walster
Production: Jenny Mulvanny
Series Consultant: Gill Matthews

ZIG ZAG

The Donkey That Was Too Fast

by David Orme

illustrated by Ruth Rivers

Evans

Gino had some coconuts
to take to the town.
He loaded them up on
his donkey.

It was a long way.

On the way he met a boy.

8

"How long will it take to get to the town?" asked Gino.

"If you go fast, it will take you a long time.

If you go slowly, you will get there quickly," said the boy.

Gino thought the boy
was silly.

13

"I have a very fast donkey. I'll get there before you," he said.

Gino and his donkey rushed along the path.

The donkey went so fast, the coconuts started to fall on to the ground.

Gino stopped for a rest.

"Where are all my coconuts?" he cried.

It took a long time to pick up the coconuts.

It was night time before
Gino got to the town.

The boy was already there.

"I told you to go slowly," said the boy.

31

Why not try reading another ZigZag book?

Dinosaur Planet　　　　　　　ISBN: 0 237 52667 0
by David Orme and Fabiano Fiorin

Tall Tilly　　　　　　　　　ISBN: 0 237 52668 9
by Jillian Powell and Tim Archbold

Batty Betty's Spells　　　　　ISBN: 0 237 52669 7
by Hilary Robinson and Belinda Worsley

The Thirsty Moose　　　　　ISBN: 0 237 52666 2
by David Orme and Mike Gordon

The Clumsy Cow　　　　　　ISBN: 0 237 52656 5
by Julia Moffatt and Lisa Williams

Open Wide!　　　　　　　　ISBN: 0 237 52657 3
by Julia Moffatt and Anni Axworthy

Too Small　　　　　　　　　ISBN 0 237 52777 4
by Kay Woodward and Deborah van de Leijgraaf

I Wish I Was An Alien　　　　ISBN 0 237 52776 6
by Vivian French and Lisa Williams

The Disappearing Cheese　　ISBN 0 237 52775 8
by Paul Harrison and Ruth Rivers

Terry the Flying Turtle　　　ISBN 0 237 52774 X
by Anna Wilson and Mike Gordon

Pet To School Day　　　　　ISBN 0 237 52773 1
by Hilary Robinson and Tim Archbold

The Cat in the Coat　　　　　ISBN 0 237 52772 3
by Vivian French and Alison Bartlett

Pig in Love　　　　　　　　ISBN 0 237 52950 5
by Vivian French and Tim Archbold

The Donkey That Was Too Fast　ISBN 0 237 52949 1
by David Orme and Ruth Rivers

The Yellow Balloon　　　　　ISBN 0 237 52948 3
by Helen Bird and Simona Dimitri

Hamish Finds Himself　　　　ISBN 0 237 52947 5
by Jillian Powell and Belinda Worsley

Flying South　　　　　　　　ISBN 0 237 52946 7
by Alan Durant and Kath Lucas

Croc by the Rock　　　　　　ISBN 0 237 52945 9
by Hilary Robinson and Mike Gordon